Chris Smithers has problems at school, with her classmates, and especially with her mom. She'd rather get in trouble than live at home, and rather get beaten up than give in to anybody. But Chris is trying to break free from all this. She just needs a little help along the way.

CHAPTER ONE

That's Life

Everyone makes mistakes. It's natural for human beings to make mistakes. We make mistakes like forgetting keys or homework, or buying milk instead of bread. But some people make mistakes that leave a mark. A mark for life, like a criminal record. And I, Christina Smithers, am one of those people.

I'm sixteen and have a record longer then my forearm. Honestly, you wouldn't expect it from me, of all people. I have dirty blond hair and kind of a baby face. I have small blue eyes and perfect white, straight teeth. I have good grades and wear nice clothes. I look like a nice kid. But I'm not. No one knows how it all started, and that's the way I wanted to leave it. But someone made me write a report on my criminal life, starting from the beginning.

I was only thirteen when I became a young offender. Before then, I was just your basic kid. My dad and I were close – I could talk to him about anything. My mom was a different story – she didn't give me any attention. That sort of upset me, but at least I had my dad. Then a brutal divorce sent my whole family through hell. I was forced to live with my mom, and I was only allowed to see my dad once a week. And then my dad was arrested for drug dealing. He already had a record, so he was sent to jail for twelve years.

I went into a tailspin: my marks, my attitude, all of it. My mom sent me to a therapist to get over it. That kind of worked. I visited dad once a month and was still near the top in my class. Then, after

three months of going to the therapist, I got a nasty surprise. I arrived in time to see my therapist kissing my mom. That's when I figured it out. I'd been sent to the therapist only because my mom had the hots for the guy.

That was the day my clean act turned dirty. I left the therapist's office and ran down the street. I ran and ran until I couldn't run anymore. When I finally stopped, the junior high was right in front of me. Tears of fury rushed down my face. I wanted to smash something – maybe the therapist, maybe my mom, maybe myself. So I picked up some stones and started throwing them at the walls of the school. When one went through the window and it set off the alarm, I wasn't scared. I just grinned from ear to ear. That smile was still on my face when the cops put me in the back of the cruiser.

It felt really good to get back at my mom. She'd disappointed me, so I'd disappoint her back. I couldn't wait to see the look on her face. Christina Smithers, nice girl, was now Christina Smithers, young offender.

But when Mom saw me in the cop car, all she did was nod. Later, after the police brought me home, she sent me to my room.

That was it! Like nothing!

After that, wanting to get back at my mother became my real goal. Rocks were easy to throw. Cars were easy to steal. And I didn't care about getting caught. I *wanted* to get caught.

So my record grew. Halfway houses became like second homes. I still got good marks at school, but it felt like school and breaking the law were the only things I was good at. Still, I was happy with the way I was. Instead of a quiet, scared little girl, I changed into a proud, loud criminal.

I liked being the new me. I liked breaking the law. Except for my dad, no one ever took any interest in my life. Well, no one except my grade ten home-room teacher, Ms. Cooper. I remember the first time she called me over after class. Shock number one – she actually wanted to listen to me. No one had asked me how I felt since I was thirteen.

It was the second week of school. We had just started again after summer break, which I had spent in a lousy halfway house. And yet, only two weeks into the term, I got arrested for putting spray-paint on the principal's car. To make matters worse, I got arrested in front of the whole school. But, then, who cares?

The principal had it in for me ever since I started at Edgemont. The very first day, I bumped into him because I was late for class. It was an accident, but the bump spilled his coffee down his pants. I did apologize, but he made me stay after school. So a week later, I snuck into his office and did a little damage. Just a little. When he found out it was me, I got a day in the bin – the room outside his office.

But the next day, Ms. Cooper stopped me outside of school. Her chestnut hair blew in the wind and her brown eyes showed interest. "Why'd you do it?" she asked me.

I knew what she meant but I pretended I didn't. I shrugged, "I don't know what you mean."

Ms. Cooper laughed in disbelief. "You know exactly what I mean. The paint on Mr. Sullivan's car? But I don't think the principal is really a skull person. He's more into smiley faces."

I looked down. I didn't know what to say.

"Actually I think he prefers the black paint that came with the car." She smiled gently at me. "Just like he prefers the stuff on his desk, not tossed on the floor."

She was still smiling.

"He's really a dull guy," she said. "Not worth all your trouble."

Ms. Cooper walked to the track behind the school. "You know where to find me if you want to talk," she said. "If you need to think, I suggest running. No doubt you're in shape. Your file says you were all-city track, once upon a time."

I said nothing. I kept remembering the times when I used to run from my dad while he chased me to take a bath. Now I run from the cops, or the teachers. Or maybe I'm just running from myself.

I'm not sure anymore.

But who was this stupid teacher asking all these questions? And why would she care about me? It just didn't make sense.

CHAPTER TWO

The Next Step

After that, Ms. Cooper was always watching me. Maybe she was waiting for me to mess up. Maybe she was a spy for Mr. Sullivan. I just couldn't figure her out.

I tried to talk to my friend, Denny, about it after school one day. But Denny wasn't listening. He was trying to explain the trouble he got into the night before. "You should have been there, Chris! It was so close! Jeremy and I were this close to getting caught," he held up his pointer finger and his thumb.

"Yeah?" I replied. Denny gets carried away a lot. If you believed him, he was *always* about to get caught for something. He was like that back in fifth grade, when we used to ride bikes together. And he was still like that.

"You know, Chris, you might like Jeremy. He's a cool guy if you give him a chance. Why won't you hang out with him? You're just like him."

I shook my head. "No way, Denny. I'm not a bit like him! Jeremy's a druggy and I'm . . . I'm just disturbed." I laughed when I said it, but that was the truth.

Jeremy was this guy who got into trouble with the law, just like me. But he got into trouble doing drugs, or beating guys up. Stupid stuff, from a stupid guy. When I became a young offender, I vowed never to touch drugs. Drugs pulled my family apart. Drugs put my dad in jail. I'd seen plenty of what drugs could do.

Denny looked down at the ground. "I meant … oh, never mind. You're right."

I nodded. I always win when Denny and I disagree. Denny thinks he's a tough guy, but he's such a pushover.

We didn't speak for a long time, then Denny got up. "What are we doing tonight, Chris? I got a new knife! You wanna have some fun with it? I see Sully got his car back. You wanna slash the tires?" Sully, a.k.a. Mr. Sullivan, our principal.

I shrugged. After talking to Ms. Cooper, I didn't feel like picking on Sully again. "Nah, he just got it back. It must have cost a lot to fix the paint after my little art class."

Denny looked at me like I had three heads. "Are you feeling okay? This is Mr. Sullivan we're talking about! You know, the guy who put you in the bin all last year! You're enemies, remember?"

I got up and walked away.

Denny followed me. We were walking toward to the car when a blond kid with really bad acne raced over to us.

"Denny! My man! What's hanging?" the kid said. Then he looked at me. "Oh, I see you found my future wife! Hey, babe."

It was Jeremy, of course. I'd met Jeremy in one of the group homes. He was a loser then and a loser now. What's worse, he was drunk. His breath reeked of alcohol – at four in the afternoon!

"Christina, baby, how are you?"

I shook my head and stood back. "It's Chris, by the way. And I was better before you arrived." I hate it when people call me Christina. That what my mom calls me. It's what my therapist called me. But decent people call me Chris.

Jeremy swayed a little. "Hmm, a little attitude! I like it. Wanna go out later, Chris?" He was slurring his words. "A hottie like you and a guy like me … it could work."

I felt like I was going to be sick. "I'd rather die, Jeremy. Now please leave. Like bye-bye. " I waved briefly, but he didn't get the message.

Jeremy grabbed my wrists and leaned in closer. "You know, they say I'm quite the kisser. You wanna try?"

I glared at him, then pulled free and shoved him away. Since he was drunk, he fell right over. I spat near his feet, then turned on my heels and stomped away.

As I was walking away from dumb and dumber (Denny and Jeremy), Ms. Cooper came out of the school. I guess she had seen the whole thing.

"Well, I guess there's some hope if you can push Jeremy away. Now he's a nasty one, but I guess you figured that out. Still, you've got a ways to go, Chris. And Denny isn't going to help you. You need new friends and new people in your life."

That did it!

"Why don't you give me a new family while you're at it?" I shot mental daggers at her. "My friends have nothing to do with my choices. Denny's my friend, the only true friend I have. And you're not taking him away. You're not taking any part of my life away. Why don't you go teach a class, or coach a team? I don't want your help . . . or your snooping! Just leave me alone!"

I was furious. How dare she talk about me and my friends? I turned away but she called after me, "I won't leave you alone until I know you're happy!"

I bolted away from Ms. Cooper, shaking my head back and forth. I ran down the laneway toward the parking lot behind the gym. Then I slowed down and started thinking. What if Denny was dragging me down? What if my friends really were a problem?

But it wasn't Denny who started it. It was my so-called mother. It was my so-called therapist. It was them, and my dad going to jail, and everything else.

With all this going on in my head, I wasn't paying much attention to where I was going. That's how I bumped into the Devil himself.

Mr. Sullivan didn't see me coming. In no time, all

his paperwork went flying. Most of it landed on the damp concrete of the parking lot.

At first old Sully acted like it was his fault. But when he realized it was me, it all changed.

"Well, well. Look who it is – my favorite student, Ms. Smithers! So what's the big hurry? You could hurt someone, or damage their property. Now pick up those papers, girl!"

What did he think I was, a slave? But I'd been in enough trouble, so I bent down and picked the papers up. Then I shoved them into his cold, clammy hands.

"Sorry for the mess, sir. I'm on my way." I tried to walk away but one hand grabbed my shoulder.

"You know, Smithers, you've been a pain in my backside ever since you arrived at Edgemont. What I'd really love to do is expel you. Can you come up with at least one good reason to keep you around?"

I looked down, trying not to laugh. I thought quickly. "Well, sir, I can actually think of three."

He raised his eyebrow.

"One, if you get rid of me, your school test scores will go down, because I am pretty smart. Two, I think Ms. Cooper would be bored if I wasn't here to bug her. And three, sir, you might get lonely in that very big office of yours. No more company from your favorite student. How would you cope?"

He laughed. "Oh, you crack me up, Smithers. If you left, I would be singing for joy in that big office."

"Ah, the sound of music," I said with sarcasm. That's the kind of stuff old guys listened to.

Sully was not amused. "Listen closely, girl. I'm only keeping you around because Ms. Cooper has asked to be your guidance counselor. She has some foolish idea that she can change you."

"Fat chance," I said.

"I agree," Sully went on. "So, starting tomorrow, you will be in our Safe School program. Everything you do, everything you might want to do, will be monitored by Ms. Cooper or by me."

He had to be lying! Safe schools – that was just a

slogan. "Safe schools, safe kids" was something the school board had come up with. It was something they did to dropouts and losers, not to kids like me.

"See you tomorrow, Christina."

Old Sully walked away, whistling to himself.

CHAPTER THREE

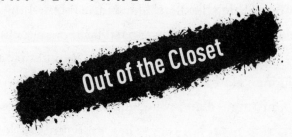

Out of the Closet

I prayed over and over again that Mr. Sullivan was lying. But when I showed up at school the next morning, Ms. Cooper was waiting for me. She gave me the big smile, the big phony smile.

"Chris, how are you this morning?"

I felt snobby. "I've been better, you know, when I was free."

"Mr. Sullivan just wants to keep you safe, Chris."

"Yeah, I'm sure," I said with real sarcasm. "So does this mean you'll be watching me all the time?"

"Something like that," she said.

"Like a jail guard?" I snapped back.

"No, like somebody who cares about you," she told me. "Now isn't that a new idea?"

I just sighed and rolled my eyes. Okay, she won that argument, but I'd get her. I'd figure out some way to get her.

"Oh, and Chris, I always win arguments," Ms. Cooper said. "It's just how I am. If you think I'll give this up because you're going to push my buttons, sorry, you're going to need a better plan."

My mouth dropped open. This woman was a freaking psychic!

"You and I both know that Denny is an offender too. So why isn't he in the Safe School thing like I am?" I asked.

Ms. Cooper shrugged. "Why bother? That boy's going to be with us for years if he doesn't get his grades up. You, on the other hand, have a great average. You're a smart girl, Chris. With a change of attitude, you might turn out not half bad someday."

Again, my mouth dropped open. (I think I'm going to dislocate my jaw at the rate I'm going!) I decided to keep my already hurting mouth shut as we walked down the hallway . . . just in case she pulled another one on me.

The only time I wasn't being followed by Ms. Cooper was when she had to teach a class or coach a team. I took advantage of that. I skipped my lunch to go hang out with Denny. He was in our usual place by the garbage bins beside the school. The garbage didn't smell, (well, only sometimes) but never enough to make us leave.

As I walked toward Denny, I saw he wasn't alone. Jeremy was with him. Jeremy was taunting him, making fun of him. Denny was trying to back away. There was a crowd of guys surrounding the two of them.

I didn't want to butt in, but I had to know what was going on. So I ducked down behind one of the bins and listened. I couldn't believe what I was hearing from Jeremy.

"What's the matter Denny? You little queer. You little ——. Aren't you staying to play? We were going to play dollies!" The crowd around Denny and Jeremy were howling with laughter.

"Would you stop it?" Denny begged.

Jeremy kept on. "Oh wait, guys, don't get too close. Denny might try to kiss you!" They all roared.

Jeremy, or someone, must have said that Denny was gay. But Denny didn't deny it. Denny had never said anything about it. But even if he was gay, so what? Whose business was it, anyway?

Besides, Denny's my best friend! My oldest friend. I wasn't going to let these idiots pull him down!

I jumped out from behind the garbage bins and lunged into Jeremy. My move took him by surprise. We both tumbled to the ground. I kept punching and kicking him like there was no tomorrow. After what seemed like ages, somebody peeled me off him. Jeremy's face was streaming with blood. I even tasted blood of my own, so I guess Jeremy got me once in the face.

Jeremy wiped his mouth, as blood dripped onto his sweater. "Oh, look who's here. Denny's best girlfriend! Are you two ladies going shopping? Maybe talk about all the cute boys who walk by?"

I struggled against the pigs holding me back. "Do you want to know something? Denny and I are friends no matter what! I really don't care if he's gay or straight or just strange." I paused for a second to get my breath. "And I don't know why *you* care, Jeremy. What does it matter to you? It's his life, not yours! Unless *you're* the one who's queer, Jeremy. Is that your real problem?"

Jeremy didn't know what to say. The witty comeback has never been his strength. Instead, he spat at Denny. Then he motioned for his pals to follow him.

"Losers," he said as they stalked away.

Denny and I were left standing beside the garbage

bins. I broke the silence when I spat out the blood in my mouth.

That's when Denny started talking. But it wasn't the same voice as the Denny I knew. This Denny was scared and shaking. "I'm sorry, Chris. I didn't think that anyone . . . would find out. I . . . I would never leave you in the dark on purpose." He was close to tears for a second, and then he began bawling.

I wrapped my arms around him and gave him a hug. "Denny, I don't care, or maybe I always knew. I mean, so what? Those idiots are the ones who were wrong. You're still my best friend."

Denny smiled.

The school buzzer went off to mark the end of lunch. Denny and I headed toward the door to get to our next class. And that was my next problem. Boy, was I in BIG trouble! My next class was P.E., and Ms. Cooper was waiting for me. She had a disappointed look on her face.

"I leave you for seventy minutes, and you get into

a fight with Jeremy Long. You even break the guy's nose! You're lucky he didn't blame you, or you'd be out of here for good."

"I broke his nose? Sweet!"

Ms. Cooper held my shoulders, not painfully, but firmly. "It's not funny! Chris! I'm trying to give you a fresh start and you throw it in my face! You're going to end up in a group home again, or worse." Then she looked me right in the eyes. "Don't you want to stay out of trouble?"

I looked down. Maybe I did, maybe I didn't. I wasn't sure about much of anything anymore.

Ms. Cooper shook her head and walked into the classroom. I could hear her voice as she talked to the rest of the class. "Today we are playing basketball. Get into teams of ten!" I moved toward a group. Basketball was one of my favorite sports. "Not you, Chris, you're running. For the whole period. Run for as long as you can!"

I was upset, but I guess I deserved it, sort of.

I started running. Ms. Cooper was right, running

is good for thinking. As I thought about the fight with Jeremy, I wondered if it was worth it. But every time I decided that it wasn't, I got mad about how he treated Denny. Jeremy was such a pig! What was his problem? He really must not have a life of his own, if he has to ruin someone else's.

After this last screw-up, I knew that Ms. Cooper wasn't going to let me out of her sight for more then a pee break. School was going to be worse than jail. It would be like getting locked into solitary.

CHAPTER FOUR

The Chase

How I survived at home was a mystery, even to me. My mother was a monster! And having Jared around didn't help. Jared was my mom's live-in boyfriend. He was also my ex-therapist . . . the pig!

I don't know much about my parents' divorce. All I know is that it had a lot to do with the bills. My mom was so serious about the whole stupid thing, and my dad would only make jokes about it. He liked to be positive about everything. You know the old saying: "Two people with the same opinion bang heads and two people with different opinions sing harmony." Well, that didn't exactly work with my parents. They were too different, in too many ways. Maybe it was my dad's drug problem that led to the divorce, but the real problems were deeper. They went back a long way, even before Jared showed up in our lives.

"Hello, Christina, how was your day?" Jared was always trying to be nice to me; I guess it was part of his training. But that didn't mean I had to be polite back.

"Just great, actually. I have a teacher who watches my every move because she has no life. And my principal is a moron just waiting for me to screw up. On the plus side, I got into a fight and broke a guy's nose! Man, I'm on a roll. You know, I think I might skip dinner. I feel like breaking some windows."

I was heading out the door when my mother grabbed my shoulder. "You're not going anywhere, Snotface." My mom calls me names all the time and "Snotface" is level one. Then we move up to the really evil, twisted names. Most of those I can't put into print. "You're going to eat dinner, and then you're going to bed. I'm sick of having the police and Mr. Sullivan on my back."

I pretended to sigh with relief. "You and me both, Mom. I promise I'll change . . . if that loser leaves my house." I pointed at Jared.

My mother slapped my across the face. I could feel the heat where her hand hit my cheek. Sure, it hurt, but I didn't back down.

"Why are you such a —," Mom began.

I cut her off before she could say the rest. "A what? A lovely daughter? Well it's because of my wonderful mother." A little more sarcasm. I don't think we had spoken straight to each other for years.

"You're a proud and nasty child!" She pulled back to strike again when I grabbed her wrist and twisted it behind her back. (See, I take notes from the cops.)

I shoved her against the wall. "Don't touch me, ever! You don't deserve to be my mother. What kind of evil monster would pay for their kid's therapist,

only to end up in bed with him? Are you even human?" I was ticked off. I tightened my grip on her wrist.

"Christina! Let go of her! Stop, stop, stop!" Jared was yelling at me, but I heard nothing. He was pulling at me, but I felt nothing except the twisting and turning of my mother. Eventually, Jared got me away from her. He flung me onto the floor and cradled my mother in his arms.

As I struggled to my feet, I could hear my mother crying, crying for attention. When Jared hushed her and hugged her, I felt like I was going to be sick.

I grabbed the door handle and left the house – no one even tried to stop me. Now I was beyond mad, I was sick. I couldn't stop my eyes filling with tears. To think that I tried to hurt my own mother! But she hit me first, she hurt me first. Four years ago, maybe she loved me. Certainly dad loved me. I had a family. Now I had nothing – nothing but a bruised cheek and blood in my mouth.

Suddenly I started blaming my dad for what had

gone wrong. Why did he have to do drugs? Why did he have to get caught? Why was he such an idiot?

But it was my mother who filed for divorce. It was my mother who didn't allow me to see my own dad. It was my mother who took up with Jared.

So I cried. I never let other people see me cry, but I was alone, so it didn't matter. I cried all the way to the park, where I sat down on a park swing. Everything in my life was going wrong. My old dreams of going to college were being blown to pieces. But I was so angry all the time, and I just couldn't control it.

I had to find a way to calm down, before it was too late. It was only a matter of time before I snapped and really hurt someone. So far, I'd only hurt me and Jeremy. But the way I felt now, anyone could be my next target.

I walked over to the playground beside my old junior high school. I ran my finger over the window I smashed three years ago, back when it all started. The window was now replaced, but it still made me think. I walked along the outside of the building. I remembered it like it was yesterday. I was furious, just like I was now. I was out of control.

I'd never been this deep in my thoughts before. I ran my finger along the old brick wall. It was rough and cold. I scratched the brick wall with my nail and hardly left a mark.

I was so deep in thought that I didn't hear people approaching until somebody spoke.

"Well, if it isn't the legend herself, Christina Smithers."

It was a bunch of jocks, and they were drunk. I didn't know any of their names. Why should I? I didn't really care about the brainless boys who were chased by cheerleaders. They weren't worth my time.

One of the jocks stepped forward. "You're hot, Christina, but you don't seem to care. I mean you dress like a guy, a guy with a bad sense of style. If you put on some decent clothes . . ."

I laughed, "Ah, fashion advice from boys who

wear spandex." I stared at them all. "Let me tell you, buying some skintight jeans and a strappy T-shirt is somewhere on my to-do list. You'll just have to wait for it." I thought a little sarcasm would shut them down.

But the leader walked up and looked me up and down. "Why you gotta be like that? Be nice and polite, baby. It's the only way the world will accept you. Of course, I'll accept you no matter what, especially if you come back to my place. How about it? The folks are out."

He was grinning, and his buddies were listening.

I let out a hollow laugh, "No thanks, guy, I'm busy tonight. Can't miss a new episode of *Prison Break*. Gotta start taking my notes sooner or later."

I tried to walk away, but he grabbed my arm, "Something more important than spending the night with me? Nothing's more important than that. Girls all over the school would kill for it."

I looked him right in the eye. "My dignity is more important, as far as I'm concerned. Thanks for the offer, but no thanks."

Still, the guy wouldn't let go.

I kept on. "Look, let's get this clear. I wouldn't go home with you if you were the last man on earth. I've never spoken to you before, and I don't even know your name!"

He grinned, "Brad, it's Brad."

"Brad … right. Well, that's different … Brad."

He perked up and loosened his grip. "Really?"

I smiled, then spat in his face and pulled my arm free. "No way, you jerk!" Then I took off, running.

I heard Brad shout after me, "Oh, she's gonna get it now! After her!"

So I had eight drunk jocks on my tail. Sure they were fast, but I had once been a track star. I also knew the Edge like the back of my hand. I easily hopped over a fence while the jocks had to stop and climb, but it didn't stop them. It gave me a head start, but now they were even angrier.

I ran through the streets not exactly knowing where I was going to end up. I turned down alleys, then back on real streets, then across an old lady's garden. I couldn't believe that the jocks were still behind me. What were they drinking? Red Bull?

I must have run about eight blocks, because I ended up at my high school. Stupid me ran right into a dead-end corner by the parking lot. I'm an idiot, I know. In no time, the jocks caught up to me. Brad grabbed me and brought his face right up to mine.

"Wrong answer, princess!"

His hand reached behind me and his lips started coming down on my mouth. Yecch. I had to do something, so I punched him in the gut.

That stopped him, but not for long.

"So you want it rough, eh?"

He came at me again, and this time I bit him – took a big hunk of skin, too. Now that really set him off. He whacked me in the face and sent my head flying to the left.

So I punched him back. The fight went on, pretty even, until his buddies came aboard. Then I was outnumbered eight to one.

They had me on the ground in no time. In the end I gave up trying to fight back and wrapped my arms around my head.

I was going to die. Or I was going to be raped. I wasn't sure which would be worse. But then I had a little good luck. There was a basketball game that night. It was just finishing up when Brad and his guys trapped me. And the back door to the gym flew open while I was on the ground. People began pouring out of the building, whooping and hollering. Obviously Edgemont had won.

So had I. The gang of jocks ran off into the darkness. I tried to stand up, but I couldn't. I tried again but someone touched me on the side. It was an accident but still I screamed in agony. I collapsed back to the ground.

The person who had bumped me looked shocked. "Sorry," he stuttered. Then got a good look at me and yelped. A girl behind him saw me and screamed. A large circle formed around my limp body. People were screaming their heads off. Eventually, a couple of teachers and Ms. Cooper showed up.

It was Ms. Cooper who sat down beside me. She was the one who started freaking out. "Chris! Oh my goodness! What happened to you?"

At that moment, I didn't know. I didn't know anything. I didn't know my name, my age or why I was on the ground with blood pouring from my nose and mouth. I didn't know a single thing.

CHAPTER FIVE

What Now?

I woke up with my head pounding and my side burning with pain. I tried to open my eyes and could only open them a crack. My mouth felt dry, like it had been caked with sand. And I didn't know where I was.

As I tried to sit up, someone at my side gasped. "Chris! Are you okay? What happened?" It was Ms. Cooper. From what I could see, it looked like I was in the hospital.

I had no clue what had happened. "Why are you

here? What happened to me?" I panicked. I didn't remember a thing. I tried to sit up again but the pain in my side made me stop and fall back on the bed. It even hurt to breathe.

Ms. Cooper tried to calm me down. "You're in the hospital because you got badly beaten up. I'm here because some people leaving the basketball game saw you. You were down on the ground, and I guess your head was the easiest target."

"A target for who?"

"I can't answer that one, Chris. But I can tell you the real reason you're here. It's because you got yourself into another situation that ended up in a fight – which you lost."

I blinked a couple of times – everything was coming back. Somehow Ms. Cooper could tell I was remembering again. So she leaned forward and raised her eyebrows. "Do you remember who did this?" I tried to catch my breath. I tried hard to remember.

"It was some jocks. I didn't know them, but one

guy . . . his name was . . . Brad. Brad, I think that was his name. He wanted me to sleep with him and I told him to beat it. He wouldn't listen, so I spat in his face and took off running. I ran to the school and got trapped in a corner. I tried to fight back, but it was hopeless. So I gave up . . . and that's all I can remember."

Ms. Cooper sat back into the chair, taken aback by my answer. "In a way I'm relieved you're here. If the guy was Brad Verba, I can tell you he's bad news, real bad news. I'm glad you stood up for yourself."

"Yeah, I guess I am, too," I mumbled.

"Anyway, your mother's here. I'll call her in. She's been up all night worried sick about you, Chris."

I tried to laugh but the only sound that came was a sob. I didn't know how much this was actually getting to me. I was sobbing, tears running from my eyes and I just could not stop. Ms. Cooper looked alarmed; she'd never seen me cry. No one had ever seen me cry.

Ms. Cooper stood there for a minute, not knowing

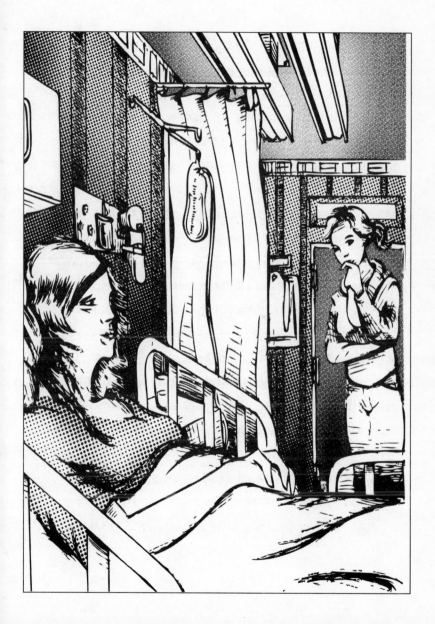

what to do, and then she figured it out. She put her arms around me and rocked me back and forth. "Chris, what's wrong?" she asked.

"Don't let my mother in! Please don't let her in. She's a monster! She doesn't want me! She hates me!"

Ms. Cooper was taken by surprise. "Does she beat you?"

"Yeah, sometimes," I said, "but that's not the worst part. It's what she says to me that hurts so much. She calls me names . . . she tells me I'm trash, I'm useless, I'm worse than useless. She doesn't care about my feelings. No one cares about what I feel."

I was calming down a bit, but I was NOT going to have my mom in the room with me. "She's treated me this way ever since Dad was arrested. Now she thinks I'm just like him, and she wants me out of her life."

I stopped and looked in Ms. Cooper's eyes. "Do you believe me?"

Ms. Cooper smiled gently and nodded. "Yes, I do.

That's why I'm going to call your mom in here so I can talk to her myself."

My mouth dropped open. "Wha . . . What?! Are you insane? She won't listen to you. She thinks she's perfect!"

Ms. Cooper opened the door. "Don't worry, Chris. I'm on your side. You'll just have to trust me."

I decided to let her make a fool of herself. She couldn't do anything to change my mom's behavior. I pulled the sheets up to cover everything but my eyes.

Finally the door opened. There was my mom, followed by Jared, with Ms. Cooper bringing up the rear. When my mom came in the room she gave me a big phony smile. Then came "the look." I knew "the look" well. It said I was worthless. It said that I should get out of her life.

But her words were something else. "Christina, what did you do this time?" She looked me over, and then acted surprised. My face was all cut and bruised and I could barely open my eyes. My dirty blond hair was flat and stringy, and I was wearing a hospital dressing gown. I didn't even know where my clothes were. What a great look for a parent-teacher conference!

Ms. Cooper smiled at my mom. "Chris didn't do anything. She was attacked outside the school and beaten."

"So who are you?" my mom snapped. "What does this have to do with you?"

Ms. Cooper caught the angry voice. "I'm Ms. Cooper . . . Christina's guidance counselor. I called for the ambulance."

My mom nodded. "So, why did you ask us to meet you here?"

My mom was sounding really stuck up but Ms. Cooper didn't back down. "According to Chris, you verbally abuse her. Is this true?"

My mom blinked and shook her head. Jared looked nervous. The two of them shared a look. "I have no idea why my daughter told you that. You told me that Christina was beaten up. I think that must have loosened a screw up there." She pointed at my swollen head.

I was angry now. "You liar!" I hissed.

Jared was sweating – he was scared and it showed. My mom looked at me with fire in her eyes.

"You liar!" I repeated. "You know you scream at me, you know you call me names, and you and I both know that you don't want me! You hate me! And guess what, mother, I HATE YOU, TOO!"

My mom looked like a steam engine with smoke coming out of her ears. "Little brat! How dare you say that to me in front of . . . a teacher! Get in the car. We're going home and we'll deal with this later. Jared, call the nurse."

"I'm not moving," I told her. I tried to set my jaw to look firm, but it hurt too much.

"Ms. Cooper, I think you should leave now," my mother said. "You've caused enough trouble."

Ms. Cooper tried to stand up, but I grabbed her arm. Then I shouted at my mother. "Don't tell her what to do. She's been more of a mother to me than you'll ever be! She cares about me! She tries to keep me in line! You just beat me and yell at me."

There was dead silence.

My mom just stared at both of us. "Well, if Ms. Cooper is so perfect, then why doesn't she keep you? You're right, Christina, I don't want you anymore. I want to start a family with Jared and you'll just get in the way. Maybe you'll be happy with the perfect Ms. Cooper . . . if she'll take a piece of dirt like you."

That's when a nurse appeared. She was looking sternly at all of us. "Please, no yelling. Other patients need their rest . . . and so do you, Ms. Smithers. Come on, now, lay back in bed. It's time for your visitors to go home." Then she turned toward my mother. "Ma'am, you can pick up your daughter tomorrow any time after noon."

My mom shook her head. "I'm busy tomorrow. Maybe my boyfriend will pick her up. Maybe." With that, my mom swept out of the room dragging Jared behind her.

Ms. Cooper just sighed as she went out. Then I was alone, alone with my thoughts.

My mom just said she doesn't want me. Oh, I see, she doesn't want me as a daughter. She just wants me as a punching bag. She wants me as a kid she can dump on. She wants me so she has somebody to pick on.

That was when I made up my mind to escape. I had to get away before anyone could come for me. Before I'd get trapped again in my mother's house.

CHAPTER SIX

Escape

There had to be a way out. Leaving the hospital at night would be stupid – the security cameras or guards would see me. If I tried going out the door or a window, an alarm would go off. So I had to escape in the morning while the hospital was busy. Then no one would notice me leaving.

So I slept, kind of, or at least rested in the bed. I kept looking at my watch to see what time it was. At seven in the morning, a nurse brought some food. I drank the juice, and then got ready to make my escape.

My first problem was the ugly hospital gown. That would be a dead giveaway. So I had to find my clothes.

I got out of bed and walked out of my room. The hospital was packed. Good. I was about to go around a corner, when a nurse appeared. "Dear, you should be in bed," she suggested.

I did my best to smile back, but it hurt. "I know, Miss. But I just need to clear my head and take a little walk around. I'll only be ten minutes, max."

She nodded and walked away. I waited until I couldn't hear her footsteps anymore and then tried to find my clothes. It took five minutes. They weren't in my room but stuck in a drawer near the nurses' station. Finally I found one wall that had patient belongings. I scrolled down to "S" and found my stuff, such as it was. My jeans were ripped and covered in mud and blood. My red T-shirt wasn't exactly red anymore. Luckily, the money I had in my jeans pocket was still there. I counted it – fifty dollars. That would be enough to buy myself some

clothes and food for about two days.

Back in my room, I quickly slipped out of the hospital gown and pulled on my clothes. Then I walked out of my room and continued down the busy corridors. There was no problem getting to the main lobby. Now to get out the door and far away, fast.

It was seven thirty and the crowd at the hospital was slowly easing. I strolled toward the front door as calmly as possible. Then I stepped through the door and out toward the parking area. I moved as fast as my sore head and painful side would let me. Finally I slowed down.

No one was following me. I was free. I came to a bus shelter. That's where I sat down, exhausted, and in no time, I fell asleep.

I woke up when the sun began to shine on me. I was still in the shabby bus shelter. It looked as though I had been sleeping there all night. I stood up and stretched my stiff body. It hurt. Oh, believe me, did it ever hurt!

I shoved my hand into my pockets and pulled out a wad of crumpled bills. I counted up and nodded. Good. It was still all there.

I knew I had to keep moving – before long someone would be looking for me. I did one last stretch, shoved my money into my jeans pocket and started walking.

Where does an unwanted girl go? There I was, a girl with a face that looked like a giant plum. What should I do? My only plan was to get out of this town, city, country, whatever. I wanted to get far away from anyone who knew me.

I'd run away before, but I always had to shoplift in order to get food. Then I'd get caught and taken straight home. But this time I had money. I figured I'd sleep on the street until my face cleared up. Then I could begin looking for a job. It couldn't be that hard to find something.

So I began walking, feeling angry and sad and scared. There was nothing for me here in Edgemont. My mother didn't love me. She didn't even want me in her house. If I thought about that, I'd start to cry. Instead, I got mad. I suddenly wished she was dead! How dare she chuck me out when I was still trying to get straight!

I felt lost and confused. I had no clue what I was going to do to survive. I had no clue what I was going to do to keep from being arrested. I needed to talk to someone who'd been on the streets like this. Somebody who could help.

As I tried to think, an old woman stopped me on the sidewalk. "Dear, do you need a lift to the hospital?"

Well, I must have looked pretty bad. I smiled and shook my head, "No thanks, Ma'am." I told her. The woman shrugged and walked on. I went quickly down the road and never looked back.

I hadn't gotten very far when I heard a voice from behind me. "Well, well, well. Christina Smithers is alive. A little beat up, but otherwise, perfectly fine."

I spun around to see who it was, but turning that quickly made me light-headed. I wobbled slightly, and was about to topple over, when rough bony hands grabbed me. I looked up to see a scrawny boy with greasy blond hair, bad acne and a bandage over his nose. Of all people – it was Jeremy! Half of me was glad to see him, and half of me wanted to run.

"Wow, hey, Chris. Easy, now. I don't want you collapse on me. Come and sit down." Jeremy led me to a park bench and sat me down.

I was surprised to see his concern. I was also surprised to see him out on the street so early. And he wasn't stoned or drunk.

"I heard about your beating last night. Who did it?"

I swallowed hard. "Brad Verba."

Jeremy shook his head. "Probably thought you'd put out for him. But that wouldn't be you, would it, Chris?"

"No, that wouldn't be me."

"And you can look after yourself. I know that better than anybody." He reached up and touched the bandage on his nose.

I offered a small smile. What was with the nice words and the good mood? Is this the same kid I had to smash in the face to rescue Denny?

"So, um, you look tired, Chris," Jeremy said.

I didn't notice Jeremy moving toward me until he was almost on top of me. "You wanna, um, come chill at my place? Just you and me." He basically breathed the last sentence in my ear.

I jumped up – carefully, this time – and stormed away.

"Hey, what's wrong?" he yelled and started to run after me.

I turned on my heels and looked him straight in the eye. I couldn't run anymore. Now I had to face things. "Jeremy, you are the biggest pig I've ever met! Sure, Brad wanted to sleep with me. He didn't pretend anything else. But you, you're making the moves just to soften me up. Acting all sweet and everything."

"Chris, don't be like that."

"But you were right. I can look after myself. I will

certainly stay away from dirty, filthy scum . . . like you, Jeremy!"

I walked as quickly as I could away from him. I made it to the parking lot before he stopped me. "You don't want to make an enemy out of me!" he told me. "You already got Brad tossed off the football team. Now you want two of us after you?"

I raised my eyebrows. "Is that a threat?"

Jeremy's hands clenched into fists. His arms were shaking. He was about to do something – grab me or hit me – but he didn't get a chance.

At that second we heard a third voice – one I knew well.

"Chris, get in the car. Jeremy, go home!" We both looked around at the voice. Ms. Cooper was leaning against her shiny black Camry.

Jeremy backed off and ran off. I let out a huge sigh.

"Where on earth do you think you're going this morning?" Ms. Cooper demanded.

"What's it to you?" I asked.

She narrowed her eyes. "Get in the car."

I shook my head. Then I said in a singsong, "Not going to happen."

Ms. Cooper stood up straight, her back stiff. "Christina, get in the damn car!"

I was shocked at her anger. I was so shocked that I actually got into the passenger seat. She got into the driver's side and started the car. We rolled out of the parking lot and sped smoothly out of the city.

I risked speaking. "Where are we going?"

Ms. Cooper had calmed down a bit. "We're going to visit someone. I set it up last night. And it would have been easier if you were at the hospital, like you should have been."

I shrugged. "Who are we going to see?"

"Your father."

CHAPTER SEVEN

A Visit

We didn't speak for the rest of the car ride. Ms. Cooper was still mad, and I had a lump in my throat.

It took us two hours on the highway to reach the prison. And then, there is was – a pile of low buildings surrounded with a wire fence that can slice skin like a knife through butter. I know – I touched it.

I was scared that I might get arrested for looking like I'd been in a gang fight. But the prison guards walked around me without giving me a second glance. I walked up to the front counter. The staff person there was on the phone, so I waited. Eventually, she hung up and looked at me.

"Visiting?"

"Uh, yes."

She shot me a look. "Visiting who?"

"Oh, my dad." I was so clueless. I was so scared.

Ms. Cooper spoke up for me. "Yes, hi. We're here for a visit with Richard Smithers. I set up the visit yesterday afternoon between Mr. Smithers and his daughter."

The woman at the counter typed on the keyboard. She looked up at me for a second time. Then she nodded and handed me a slip of paper. "Your dad will be waiting there for you."

My hand was shaking as I held the paper in front of me. I hadn't seen my dad in four years. What if he didn't recognize me? Not that I could blame him – the way my face looked at the moment. But even if my face was swollen, he should be able to recognize his own daughter. Then there was the other awful question. What if he didn't want to see me? What if he had turned against me, like my mom?

At last, Ms. Cooper and I found the visiting room. Men in ugly orange uniforms were all busy talking to their visitors, but one man was sitting alone, waiting.

I recognized my dad right away. He had the same dirty blond hair, big green eyes and muscular arms as before. It was him, my dad, my best friend. I grinned and ran to the glass barrier. He saw me coming and beamed. Then he jumped up and held his arms open as if he could give me a hug despite the glass.

We were together again.

My head started to spin, either from the fight, or maybe just from seeing my dad. We sat there for the longest time without saying a word. I missed him so much. And there was so much to say. Where could I start? How much should I tell him?

But it was my dad who started the talk. He bent to the microphone and asked his big question. "Chris! What happened to you?"

I shrugged. "Got into a fight. No big deal. How've you been?" I didn't really want to discuss the whole fight thing. I wanted that kind of stuff left behind me, buried in the past. Besides, I wanted to find out how my dad was.

"As good as any guy in jail, I guess. And you? We haven't seen each other in a long while. Why haven't you come to visit?"

I was close to tears. "I've missed you so much, dad. That horrible monster who calls herself my mother banned me from seeing you ever again. But I don't care anymore. I don't live with her anymore. She kicked me out. She doesn't want me. I'm stay . . . well, I'm going to work something out. Anything that will get me away from Mom. This is Ms. Cooper by the way. She's my guidance counselor."

My dad looked confused. "Hi, nice to meet you," he said, nodding to Ms. Cooper. She nodded back but Dad had already turned to me.

"She kicked you out? But you're sixteen! Where does a sixteen-year old go, when there's no home for them?" I nodded in agreement. I loved having someone to talk to who understood me. I love how my dad doesn't push anything that's bothering me. He trusts me to work it out. That's what good parents do, isn't it?

"You know, Tina, I've been told that if I keep my nose clean, I will get out early. Maybe even before your eighteenth birthday!"

My eyes shot wide open, "Really?!"

"Really," he said, his eyes smiling.

We spent a lot of time talking about what we were going to do later, when my dad walked out of prison as a free man. We talked about going to the movies, going fishing, watching *American Idol*, you know, all the father-daughter things. We also had to discuss school. I told him I was still doing well, and then I had to admit the rest.

I came clean. I told him about my feelings about Mr. Sullivan. I told him I only have one friend, a boy who happens to be gay. Then, at last, I told him all about Ms. Cooper. I told him all about Ms. Cooper's conference with Mom and how she put Mom in her place. I said how she is so much fun after you get to know her.

I think I embarrassed Ms. Cooper a bit. She kept looking away whenever I bragged about her to Dad.

Still, I think Dad liked her. She was definitely better at keeping me alive than Mom was.

Dad and I chatted a while more, but then, sadly, our time was up. The officer told us that my dad had to go back to his cell. We promised to have another visit at the end of the week. But before leaving, he said he had a request.

"Christina, I know this is hard, but, please, don't give up on yourself. Things will sort themselves out soon. I promise." It was sad for me to agree, but he was right.

"Okay, Dad. I love you." He nodded and smiled as the guard led him away.

CHAPTER EIGHT

Framed

Ms. Cooper and I walked out of the prison together and headed for her car. As soon as we were both inside, I burst into tears. I didn't even know this woman very well, yet here I was crying in her arms.

I was so happy about my dad. He was going to be free! In a year and a half, I could live with him again. My mother would be out of the picture for good. And so what? She's got Jared. What more could she possibly need? For me, everything was looking up. It was a new beginning to my life.

I woke up in the spare room of Ms. Cooper's house. The two of us didn't do much talking the night before. We ate silently, I had a shower, and then I went to bed. That morning Ms. Cooper drove me to school and said she would keep on looking out for me. She said I could stay at her house, at least until things were sorted out.

So I didn't do anything against the rules all day. Actually I didn't break any rules for the rest of the week. Mr. Sullivan still didn't accept that I had changed. He asked me to come to his office with Ms. Cooper on Friday. We entered his office and sat down in front of him in the comfy, squishy chairs.

"Well, Ms. Smithers, according to Ms. Cooper, you've been very good the past week. Not even any problems outside of school, at least none that we've heard of. Have you changed or are you just trying to get on my good side so you're free to do what you want?"

I looked up into his eyes. "No, sir. I have no interest in my old life. I promised my dad I'd change. And I am one who keeps my promises."

Ms. Cooper chimed in. "Yes, I believe Christina doesn't need my supervision at school anymore. I think she is ready to look after herself. What about making next week a trial week, where she can be without supervision? If she acts out, then I'll come back in. If she doesn't, she's free."

Mr. Sullivan shook his head. "I agree about next week being a trial. But here's my deal. If she acts out, even once . . . she's out."

"Out?" asked Ms. Cooper.

"Out … expelled," he said, turning to look at me with those icy cold blue eyes. "No more chances. Goodbye Christina. If you've started a new life, stick with it. Deal?" He held out his hand to me.

I had to think about it for a second, but what choice did I have? I nodded and shook his hand. "Deal."

At lunch, I headed for the garbage bin area where Denny and I used to hang. It was stupid, but I did it.

Luckily, I found Denny there. His brown hair was blowing in the wind. He was leaning awkwardly on the dumpster and looking at his feet.

"Hey man, looking for something?" I asked him.

Denny looked up at me and broke into a grin. "Chris! You're free! How'd you do it?"

I smiled and walked over to him. "I was good. No more acting out for this girl. I'm done. You wanna join me on the straight side? It's a lot more fun."

Denny looked away, thinking, then he turned to me and smiled. "Is it really more fun? No more running from Sully and the cops? That's really fun?"

I laughed. "Yeah, it is. You get more respect. And you kind of feel better about yourself."

He nodded. "I trust you, Chris, so I'll give it a try. But we're still a team, right?"

I nodded and gave him a hug. "Definitely, starting with your grades. I'm going to tutor you."

So Denny and I started helping out around the school, staying late so I could tutor him, but we still hung out as buds.

All that time, I still slept at Ms. Cooper's. My mom really didn't want me back, so where else could I go? I mean, it was there or a group home, and I didn't want to deal with that again.

Even though Ms. Copper is single and lives by herself, we did lots of mother-daughter things. We went shopping, we went out for dinner, we went bowling. One day we even went to see a sappy chick-flick together. We also made regular visits to my dad. Ms. Cooper trusted me and respected me, which is more than I can say about my actual mother.

But then something happened that pushed our friendship to the edge.

Monday came all too quickly, and I wasn't planning to do anything stupid. I wanted freedom. But clearly, freedom didn't want me. Or other people didn't think I deserved freedom – those people being Jeremy and Brad. Yeah, the druggy and the jock teamed up to keep me from being free. Actually, they didn't even want me alive.

I was walking to my second class when I ran into a huge mob of students. People were laughing, gasping, and yelling at the top of their lungs. I fought through the crowd and ended up at the center of it all.

The walls outside the cafeteria were covered in graffiti. There was a cartoon drawing of Mr. Sullivan smoking a cigarette and holding a porn magazine. The huge cartoon head had a very large, sloppy grin on its face and a speech bubble that said, "I like to blow bubbles in my free time!"

No one could come up with something better? I mean, what kind of idiot would paint this stuff on the wall?

That's when it happened. Somebody stuck a paintbrush in my hand. And, before I could do anything, a bright flash shone in my eyes.

"Caught at the scene of the crime." It was Brad Verba, and he was holding a camera.

Then some girl joined in with Brad. "It was her! I saw the whole thing! Then she threatened me if I told." She pointed at me, grinning like crazy. "It was her!"

I started to shake my head no. I threw the brush away and started to explain . . . when Ms. Cooper showed up.

Poor Ms. Cooper just looked at me with her mouth open. She gave me a look that said she wasn't gonna pull me out of this one.

And I didn't even do it!

"Ooh, the real Christina Smithers is back," some teacher called out. "I thought it was too good to be true! Clear the hallways!" The school cop came out and dragged me down to Mr. Sullivan's office.

In came Mr. Sullivan and Ms. Cooper. Mr. Sullivan walked straight to his desk and pulled out some paperwork.

"You're expelled," he said, almost smiling as the words came out.

"But that's not fair. I didn't do it!"

Mr. Sullivan swung around on his heels and looked directly into my eyes. "Oh, really? Well it seems we have a witness and a photograph. You're not getting out of this one, Smithers."

Even Ms. Cooper agreed. "That was the deal Chris," she said with a sigh. "That was the deal."

"Wait! You can't do this," I begged. "I was set up! It was Brad and Jeremy! I was in math class the whole morning! I didn't go to the john – I didn't go anywhere. Ask Mrs. Kieran! I was nowhere near that hallway. Please believe me!"

Ms. Cooper jumped up and grabbed my wrist. "Are you positive?"

I nodded so she turned to look at Mr. Sullivan.

He sighed and shook his head. "Fine, I'll look into this. But until we get this sorted out, you're suspended. I have a picture of you, Ms. Smithers, with a paintbrush in your hand, young lady. So somebody has to give me a better explanation of how that 'art' got up there. In the meantime, go home until we figure this out."

Mr. Sullivan walked up to me and stuck his face close to mine. "And if I find out you're lying, there won't be a school in the country that will take you. So help me."

I stared directly into his cold eyes. "I swear on my life that I didn't do a thing."

The school cop walked me to Ms. Cooper's car with her and waited while I got in. Then he shook his head as I slumped in the seat.

Ms. Cooper and I made the drive in silence. Then Ms. Cooper dropped me off at her place and looked at me with piercing eyes. "You better not be lying, Chris," she said with a voice that was sharp and cold.

I actually felt ashamed for something I didn't do. But why? It must have been Ms. Cooper's voice or the look in her eyes. For the first time, ever, I felt she didn't trust me.

CHAPTER NINE

Revenge

I was nervous the next morning. I kept pacing around the little house, wondering if Ms. Cooper could get at the truth. I was ready to go for a walk when my cell phone rang. It was Denny.

"Chris, I gotta see you."

"No problem," I replied. "I've got the day off. Maybe I've got lots of days off unless Sully believes me."

"Oh, he believes you, Chris," Denny replied, coughing into his cell phone. "But I've got to see you. It's, like, important."

"So where are you?"

Denny's voice was funny, so I could barely hear what he said. It seemed odd that he'd be in an alley south of the school, but that's what he said. So I grabbed my coat and headed off.

I found the alley just off Locust, but couldn't see Denny. The alley was kind of creepy, so I called out his name a couple of times. Then I heard an answer. It was my name, but kind of muffled.

So I walked down the alley slowly, still calling out Denny's name. I had just got behind the old Morton's store when I saw another alley – and Denny's legs sticking out of a doorway.

"Denny!" I screamed. I ran over to where he lay on the ground.

And that's when I saw the rest of them. Brad and Jeremy held my friend in a headlock. It was so tight that Denny could barely breathe.

"Let him go!" I shouted.

It was a setup. They'd forced Denny to make the call to get to me – and it worked.

"Look, Denny, your angel has arrived," Brad said with a laugh.

Denny couldn't speak. His face was white and he was struggling to breathe.

I heard laughter from behind me. I turned around, but, lucky me, I swung right into a fist. The fist knocked me off my feet.

Jeremy look down at me with a sick smile. "So, you think you can just change overnight, Chris? One minute you're the queen of evil, next you're sucking up to Cooper and Sullivan. Sounds a bit pathetic if you ask me."

I scrambled to my feet, but then big beefy arms grabbed me from behind. I didn't know the guy holding me, but by his stench I could tell he was a jock.

"You're the pathetic one, Brad. You just had to get me expelled, didn't you? So you two painted the hallway and paid some stupid ninth grader to say it was me."

"So clever of you to figure it out," Jeremy sneered.

"But here's your problem – Sullivan figured it out too. He says you ratted on us."

"And that's the second time, Chris," Brad added. "The first time, you got me kicked off the football team."

"So we owe you, Chris," Jeremy said. "And we're going to get even – starting with your friend."

Brad tightened his arm around Denny's neck.

"Let him go! You're going to kill him!"

Brad released Denny and threw him to the ground. Another jock walked up to Denny and kicked him as he lay there.

I had to do something, and fast. So I elbowed the boy holding me, hard, in the gut, and got out of his grip. Then I lunged at the ground where a glass wine bottle lay. I picked it up and smashed it against the wall. Pieces of broken glass flew in all directions; one piece even hit some jock in the leg. The guy collapsed and cradled his thigh.

I swung the broken wine bottle around to face the rest of them.

Jeremy and Brad faced me with fire in their eyes. "You just got us mad, Chris."

I gritted my teeth. I wasn't thinking about getting them mad; I was thinking about staying alive. There were four of them and just one of me, but at least I had a weapon.

Then Jeremy pulled out a knife and Brad pulled out a gun. Suddenly my weapon didn't count that much.

I dropped the wine bottle. It smashed into pieces on the concrete.

"Good choice, princess," Brad hissed between his teeth.

I backed away from the four guys. I looked over at Denny and saw him lying unconscious on the ground. There was blood trickling from his mouth. I looked back at Jeremy and Brad. I tried to show I wasn't afraid, but in doing so, I noticed something that almost made me laugh. The gun in Brad's hand was a fake, a toy. It was about as lethal as a block of Lego.

Brad came forward and pushed the empty pistol against my forehead. "If I were you, I'd give up. There's no way you're getting out of this."

I looked him right in the eyes. "If you were me," I narrowed my eyes, "you'd be way smarter than you are."

Brad tightened his finger on the trigger.

"Brad, do you play poker?"

He looked confused. "Yeah, I do."

I grinned and pushed the pistol away from my face. "Then maybe you should take some lessons in bluffing. Your gun is a toy, Brad. It looks like you got it from a cereal box."

I've never seen someone look so stupid in my life. Brad threw the pistol to the ground just as I took a swing at his jaw.

Then Jeremy lunged toward me, slicing at the air with his blade.

I swerved out of the way, but then I felt a sharp stinging pain in my forearm. I tripped and fell to the ground, broken glass sticking into my hands. I rolled onto my back just in time to see Jeremy lunging at me again. Quickly I held up my arms and grabbed his wrists. For a few seconds, we were wrestling on the ground with the knife between us.

After what seemed like an eternity, I was able to flip over and get on top of Jeremy. During the roll, the knife dropped. It lay on the ground beside us. I reached to grab it, but felt a hard blow right to my stomach. Brad had kicked me in the gut. I fell off Jeremy, trying to catch my breath.

That's when the other two guys yanked me up. They held my arms behind my back. I struggled and tried to pull free, but it was useless. I was too weak. They were too strong.

Jeremy stood up and walked toward me. Then he swung his right fist at my head. Then it was Brad's turn, a punch that made my jaw crunch. Soon it was blow after blow. Blood gushed out my nose and mouth, but I was still alive. Even though my eyes were bleeding, I could still see.

This is the end. I'm being tortured for wanting to

change my life. That's what I thought as Jeremy and Brad circled me like vultures. They kept kicking my legs, arms and gut.

And then it started raining. Soon I was lying in the middle of a red puddle of blood and water. I could hear laughter coming from the guys above me. I could hear the thunder rumbling up in the sky. I could feel rain pounding cold and wet on my body.

I could feel and hear all of this, but at the same time, I couldn't hear or feel a thing. A bright light shone in my eyes, blinding me. *The light,* I thought, *the last thing you see before you die. This really is the end. And I never had a chance to say goodbye.*

CHAPTER TEN

Home Again

The bright white light was shining in my eyes. I looked around. Is this Heaven? "Christina." I looked to the right. "Christina." I looked to the left. "Christina." Now I looked straight ahead. There was no one in sight, but why could I hear someone's voice? "Christina! Please wake up! "Christina!" The bright light went out, and I was in darkness.

I blinked. I could hear voices all around me. "We don't know when Christina will come out of this. We're not even sure if she will wake up at all."

I blinked twice and tried to speak, but I had some sort of tube down my throat. So I tried to make a grumbling sound. I could see Ms. Cooper and Denny at the bottom of my bed. They were talking with someone wearing a white jacket, but they couldn't hear me.

Ms. Cooper looked worried and Denny was white as a ghost. They talked. They looked at me and I blinked again. Then I tried to wave my arm back and forth.

Denny saw it first. "Ms. Cooper! Look!" He darted to my side, followed closely by Ms. Cooper.

My arm fell down on the bed and I felt weak, like my arm was spaghetti. Nothing would move at all anymore. The doctor came up to my other side to check my monitor. Then he took the tube out of my throat, making me gag for a second.

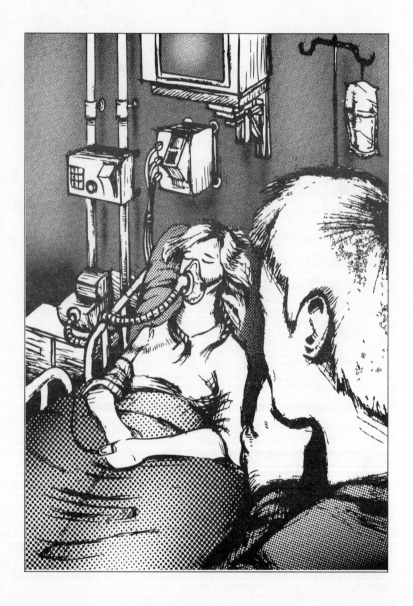

"Chris!" Denny said, shaking my arm.

I tried to speak back, but my mouth was as dry as sandpaper. Ms. Cooper gave me a sip of water. That helped.

I sat up and looked at the two of them. Ms. Cooper looked like she was ready for her sixtieth birthday, with big, saggy bags under her eyes. Denny just looked like he had seen a ghost.

"What happened to me?" I asked.

Ms. Cooper stroked my hair. "You were attacked, Chris. You've been in a coma for three weeks."

Denny looked close to tears. "I was out cold, Chris. There was nothing I could do . . . nothing. I'm good for nothing!" And then Denny burst into tears.

Ms. Cooper grabbed his shoulder. "You did your best. If you hadn't grabbed her cell phone to call the cops, Chris would have died."

I looked over to Denny. "The bright light. It wasn't me dying. It was a patrol car, wasn't it?"

Denny nodded. Then all three of us burst into

tears. People always said that Denny was good for nothing. But now we all knew . . . We all knew that Denny was good for something. He was good at keeping me alive.

I was allowed to come home a week after that. The doctors named me "The Miracle Girl" because I came back after being in a coma for so long. I stayed at Ms. Cooper's house, just like before. After a week of doing nothing, Mr. Sullivan allowed me to attend school again. Back at Edgemont, I was a hero, I guess. Or maybe a victim. People patted me on the shoulder. Girls I didn't know came up and told me I had been brave. Maybe I was; I still don't remember.

Brad and Jeremy were arrested for assault, along with the nameless guys who helped. The charge might have been murder, except I didn't die. They're all sitting in jail now.

So I went back to school while I waited for the court case. Pretty soon, my marks were back up.

And Mr. Sullivan got over my stupid past and accepted me for who I was. I wasn't in the Safe School program anymore. I was just me, Christina Smithers, formerly screwed-up student.

Here's the funny part – it turns out that Jared dumped my mother. When I heard that, I laughed so hard that I cried. I guess Jared didn't like the way my mom treated me, so the thought of having kids with her scared him. Jared even came to see me and apologize. My old therapist gave me a "get well soon" card. Can you beat that? Maybe the guy was just poisoned by my witch of a mother. I still can't forgive him for using me to get to my mother, but I'm trying.

I also got a new therapist, with a new approach. Instead of beating myself up to get back at my mother, maybe I should take on my mom. So I did. I charged my mother with verbal and physical abuse. While all that was in the courts, I needed a guardian. I was still only sixteen, turning seventeen. Since my dad wasn't getting out until later, the court chose

Ms. Cooper to look after me. She ended up being my foster mother. Every morning, Ms. Cooper and I would go for a run before school. It helped work out the stuff, all the stuff still inside me.

Ms. Cooper took me to visit my dad every week. And when Ms. Cooper was busy, I got on the bus and went by myself. Yes, I was still trying to give up doing stupid things. After you've done that for three years, it's kind of like a really annoying bad habit. But I'm working on it.

Denny and I were still close. Once he came to terms with it, nobody else cared that he was gay. And Denny seemed to feel a lot better now that everybody knew. He felt better about being himself – something I was still working on.

So Denny was a changed guy. On Tuesday we would walk from school and help out at the animal shelter. Wednesday, we would pick up garbage around the school. Thursday he'd go tutor at the rec center. And the police were slowly taking some ticks off our records.

As well as visiting my dad, I tried to visit my mom, too. But she refused to see me. I was hurt, deep down. But I had other people around who cared about me. I had Dad, who was going to come home soon. I had Ms. Cooper who fed me and put a roof over my head. I had Denny who loved me as a really good friend.

And, believe it or not, I even had Mr. Sullivan on my side. Sully grew to trust me. He even used me as a model for younger students, although some of the kids were still scared of me. When I'd go visit a junior high, some of those kids would come up and tell me the crazy things they did. So I sit them down and tell them what I'd figured out.

I always tell them, "Everyone makes mistakes. It's natural for human beings to make mistakes. We make mistakes like forgetting keys or homework, or buying milk instead of bread. But some people make mistakes that leave a mark. A mark for life, like a criminal record. And I, Christina Smithers, am one of those people."

Epilogue

Today is my eighteenth birthday. I've been living with Ms. Cooper for a year and a half now. I'm graduating at the end of the year and going to college next fall. My dad was released from prison yesterday and I'm moving in with him tomorrow.

My life has been so different these last couple of years. I've lived in happiness – such a strange thing. No fighting. No arguing. Just waking up happy to be alive.

Denny and I have been telling kids our stories. I go to schools and tell the students the same things over and over. Don't beat up on yourself to get back at your parents. It's simple. Really.

I guess that near-death experience really freaked me out. Every time I think about it, I scare myself. I keep asking myself, "Was it all really worth dying for?" The answer is no.

Somehow I got addicted to breaking the law. That was the old Chris, the one who got in trouble. But trouble is just like smoking. You've got to break the habit sooner or later.

Ms. Cooper – I call her Catherine now – has taken such good care of me. I'm going to miss living with her, living in this little house. But for the next six months, my dad will have to stay in jail on weekends. That means I'll get to stay over with Ms. Cooper. Until I graduate that is.

My life has changed so much. But deep down, I know I'm the same girl I was five years ago, before any of this happened. Before the divorce, before

Jared, before the acting out, before the halfway houses. Before anything. I'm still the same person I used to be. I'm Christina Smithers, and I always will be me.

That's all people need to be: themselves.

Check out these other EDGE novels

Behind the Door by Paul Kropp. Jamal and his buddies like to hang out in the basement of an old warehouse. Things are cool until a strange door appears on an inside wall. Of course, the guys have to look behind the door — and then the horror begins.

Outrage by Tony Varrato. Connor's had a rough day — punched out by a buddy, kicked out of school, beaten up on the way home. And then he gets accused of robbing a corner store. It all sucks, big time.

Turf War by Alex Kropp. Kasim and his friends aren't much of a gang. They're not like Crips or Bloods, they're just a bunch of guys who hang togther. But that doesn't stop the Parkside Prep guys when they decide to clean up the Edge.

If you enjoyed this book, check out this excerpt from
The Bully

CHAPTER 2

That Was Then, This Is Worse

Danni began to bully me back in Grade 7. That was four years ago. It still gives me shivers when I think back. Danni Heller was the worst bully in our school — and she was a girl.

You read about *boy* bullies all the time. Your hear how they choose a victim. How they choose some kid who's smaller and weaker than they are. You hear how they pick on the kid, day after day. You hear about all the physical stuff — the pushes, the punches, the kicks.

But girl bullies aren't like that. A girl bully won't beat you up. A girl bully won't push you up against a schoolyard fence. A girl bully doesn't do that much physical stuff. Instead, she beats up your brain. She makes you so scared that you wake up each day just ready to cry.

I know — I was the victim. Danielle Heller was the bully.

It didn't make sense when it all started. Danni and I had been best friends when we were little, but then things got messed up. It wasn't even her fault. Danni's stepdad got thrown in jail for robbing a gas station. After that it didn't seem like Danni cared about school . . . or much of anything. She started hanging out with tougher, older kids at school. I heard she took up smoking and drinking, way back when she was still a kid.

Of course, my life had changed, too. Caitlin moved in across the street, and she was a lot more fun to be with. We played tennis and told

jokes and read the same books. Danni moved off to a new group of kids. Caitlin and I became best friends.

Maybe Danni didn't like that. Maybe she was jealous when Caitlin became my friend. Maybe she thought that Caitlin and I looked down on her — that we were stuck up. Or maybe I'm just blaming myself. They say that victims do that. We blame ourselves for what the bully does.

The problem between Danni and me really started at school. We were in the girls' bathroom with our new lipsticks, trying to look "beautiful." Then Danni took her lipstick and wrote a couple of swear words on the walls. She started laughing. It was like the swear words were the biggest joke in the world. I told her to cut it out because I didn't want to get in trouble. Then Danny put a big streak of lipstick on my cheek. I couldn't believe it! She had this strange look on her face. It was like she was angry at me or proud of herself, or something.

So I ran out, rubbing the mark off with a tissue.

I knew that Danni was having trouble at home. I knew she was hanging out with a tough crowd. So I didn't blame her, that day. I didn't tell our teacher, or anyone, what had happened.

But Danni still got caught. I think the principal knew who did it all along. I know he called me into the office, but I kept my mouth shut. I'm not a rat — really, I'm not. But somehow Danni got nailed for the mess. She was suspended for a few days, and then it got worse. Her mom kicked her out of her house for a week.

When Danni came back to school, she blamed me. She said that I was a rat. She said I was the *only* one who could have told on her. And the word began to spread. We weren't friends any more, and I was a rat.

When we all came back to Grade 8, I thought it would be over. I thought that Danni would forget over the summer. But I was so wrong! Grade 8 was the year Danni turned mean. It was all little stuff — a note passed in class, a nasty word, a mean look on her face. I was being bullied, but no one could see it.

My friend Caitlin said I was too sensitive. She said I should ignore all the stuff. But I couldn't. Danni had been my friend, and now she was making trouble for me. She kept it up, day after day. It kept on until Christmas — and then Danni was gone.

Nobody knew where Danni had gone. The

word was that her mom and stepdad broke up. Some kids said that Danni had to move with her mom. But other kids said that Danni had been kicked out again, for good. Nobody knew for sure.

But nobody was as glad as I was. My life got back to normal. I could stop looking over my shoulder. I could walk down the hall or head to the bathroom without worrying. I became the normal, happy kid I used to be.

Until Danni came back. Until Danni came back to mess up my life again.

*　*　*

I felt better when the last buzzer rang at school. All day I had been mad at Justin. I did my best to avoid him. At lunch I saw him waiting for me at my locker, so I turned and walked to the pizza place next door. I grabbed a slice of pizza and ate by myself. I didn't want to talk to him. I didn't want to get into another fight.

I guess I didn't feel like talking to anyone. At the end of classes, I grabbed my stuff and walked out the school's back door. I would have met Caitlin, but she was at a soccer practice. That left me walking home by myself.

I didn't get that far. Danni was waiting at the street that led to my house. I thought about turning back. I could pretend that I'd forgotten something at school. But that would just make it worse. If she was going to do something, I might as well face it.

"Well, if it isn't the rat," Danni said, as I came close.

"Hello, Danni," I said, trying to keep cool.

I wanted to keep walking, to get home, but Danni stepped in front of me.

"I hear you've got your claws into Justin," she said.

"He's my boyfriend," I said.

"For now," Danni told me, her tone carrying the threat. "Maybe he's your boyfriend *for now*, but things can change just like . . . " and then she snapped her fingers.

"Not Justin," I said.

"Yeah, you just keep hoping," Danni snapped back. "I know what guys like, Allie, even nice boys like Justin."

I didn't want to hear any more. I pushed past her and walked quickly down the street.

Danni shouted after me. "Next time you kiss him, Allie, make it a good one. Because you'll be kissing him goodbye."

Jennifer Mulrine is a high school student in Mississauga, Ontario, Canada. She began this book while still in grade 8 and submitted the manuscript to HIP's senior editor Paul Kropp when he was visiting her school. The editors at HIP thought the rough manuscript showed unusual promise, and worked with Jennifer to expand and develop the book so it would be suitable for the Edge series. *Breaking Free* is Jennifer Mulrine's first published novel. When she completes high school, she intends to continue writing novels and go to university to take up journalism. In addition to writing, Jennifer enjoys horseback riding, swimming, and reading other great books.

NO TEACHERS ALLOWED:

For online discussion of HIP Edge novels and characters, student readers are invited to the HIP Edge Café.

www.hip-edge-cafe.com

For more information on HIP novels:

 High Interest Publishing – Publishers of EDGE novels
407 Wellesley Street East • Toronto, Ontario M4X 1H5
www.hip-books.com